An Unexpected Love

By

Lizzy Stevens

And

Steve Miller

Chapter One

As Olivia drove away in her little red convertible the world would have thought her life was perfect. In reality though; nobody ever really knows the full truth of somebody else's life. She drove away tears running down her cheeks and her hand on her stomach shielding her unborn baby from the horrible life it would have lived had she stayed. She knew there wasn't a life for her there. They wouldn't fit into the lifestyle of the former high school football star turned big time frat boy in college. Where does a baby fit into drunken parties full of beer pong and chaos? She had to get away. She knew she had to leave before Chris ever found out about the baby. He wasn't father material. She wouldn't force a child on him and she wouldn't force him on a child. Her child deserved a father who actually wanted to be a father.

"Olivia felt a pang of guilt over the note she'd left him."

"Dear Chris,

I know this will probably come as a shock to you but I don't love you anymore. I'm sorry to be so blunt about it, but I don't fit into your busy football life any longer. I'm leaving school for now. I'm not sure what I want to do with my life at the moment. I've thought long and hard about this and I'm sorry if I hurt you. I wish you all the best in life.

Always,

Olivia

She really didn't know what she was going to do or where she was going to go, but for starters the best thing for her was to go home to her father. She knew that he would have answers for her. The road stretched for hours before the familiar security gate came into view. A solitary guard greeted her.

"Hello Ms. Vandergate. How are you this evening?"

Olivia knew she must look a mess after crying most of the way, but she didn't care. Keeping her voice steady, she said. "I'm great. Thanks."

The guard allowed her to pass with a wave, and she drove up the long winding drive to the beautiful white Victorian style house with white columns. Her family was what people called 'old money.' Her grandfather owned most of the town and, after he died, everything went to her father who ended up buying most of the rest of the town. They were a very prominent family which meant telling her father that she had a scandal wasn't going to go over very well. He wouldn't like the fact that his only daughter was pregnant out of wedlock and had no plans to marry the father of the child. This type of news wasn't exactly the kind of thing that was easy to tell her father.

As Olivia rubbed her hands on her jeans nervously and then quickly pulled her hair back in a ponytail. She did one last rub of her eyes to make sure they weren't too badly tear stained before walking into the house.

"Hello Ms Olivia." The Butler greeted her.

"Hello Winford. I'm going to go in and see Daddy." She walked over and gently knocked on the door of her father's study.

She heard a voice on the other end of the door say to come in. As she stood there with trembling hands she slowly turned the knob.

"Olivia. Darling come on in. I wasn't expecting you today."

"Hi Daddy." She said trying not to unleash the waterworks but it didn't work. They came flooding down and she found herself crying uncontrollably.

Her father hurried to her side and put his arms around her. "What is it? What happened? Are you okay?"

Olivia wiped away the tears and looked at her father. "Daddy. I'm in trouble. I need your help."

They walked over to couch to sit and talk. Olivia sank down into the cool brown leather as memories rushed through her head. She had more talks than she could remember with her father on that very couch.

David Vandergate was a very understanding man when it came to his only daughter. He would do anything in his powers to help her and Olivia knew that.

"What is it, Honey? Just tell me and I'll make it better."

Olivia took a deep breath then let it out slowly. "Daddy, you were right about Chris. All he wanted to do was party every night. Other than football of course."

David looked at his daughter with a little bit of confusion. "Okay. Hold on. You are this upset because of a fight you had with your boyfriend. That doesn't sound like you."

As she scratched her head and tried to find the right words, she started to fill him in on the whole story. "I wish that was all Daddy. I thought things were going to be different. I knew how he was in high school but I thought now that he was an adult that things would change. Well I learned fast that things didn't change. He is still acting like a child with no care about the future. He has no plan at all if he doesn't get drafted into the NFL. I have more to think about than just me now. I have my child to think about." She sat there for a minute waiting for her father to understand what she just told him.

"Your child? Olivia, what are you saying?"

"I'm pregnant Daddy."

David got up and started pacing back and forth in his study. He ran his hand through his smoky gray hair looking for the words. "Does he know about the baby?"

Olivia began to cry. "No! I couldn't tell him. He is no kind of father. What would we do? Show up on weekends with our baby to his frat party?"

David walked to his daughter and put his arm around her. "Okay good. I'll fix this. You tell nobody that you are pregnant until I say. Don't worry. I will take care of everything. You go get some rest and we will talk tomorrow." He kissed his daughter on the forehead before leading her out of the study.

Olivia walked out of the study mentally exhausted. She knew her father would know what to do. She walked up the stairs to her bedroom to get some clothes before going to take a long hot bath. She stood in the middle of the room looking around. Her father had kept it exactly the way she left it. Her Bon Jovi poster was on the wall right where she left it. She smiled as she thought about the huge crush she had on him. Not unlike most girls her age, her nights were filled with dream after dream of marrying him. She walked over and picked up her pom poms from her cheerleading days thinking of how things were much easier back then. She dropped them back down on the dresser and her hand landed on her stomach. How was she supposed to raise a child when she wasn't much more than one herself?

She gathered her clothes and went to the bathroom and started the hot water. She poured her favorite scent of bubble bath into the water before getting in. As she sank down in the steamy hot bubbles she wished her mother was still alive to talk to. Her father was wonderful but at times a daughter likes to talk to her mother. Sometimes a mom's shoulder to cry on is what she needed.

Olivia stayed in the water until it turned cold then got out and wrapped herself in her big white fluffy robe. She was completely worn out and fell asleep the minute her head hit the pillow.

Chapter Two

The next morning Olivia woke early, got up and dressed before going down to meet her father. It had been a long restless night but she had managed to get a few hours' sleep. Thoughts of Chris ran through her head. She had left him with not much of an explanation. She couldn't help but feel as if she took the coward's way out. She glanced in the mirror at the bags under her eyes and tried to cover them with make-up the best she could. She ran the brush through her long brown hair before pulling it back in a hair tie. *Well this is as good as it's going to get.* She thought but knew that wasn't going to be acceptable. She grabbed her make-up bag and got to work on making herself presentable before going downstairs.

When she got to the bottom of the stairs she heard voices coming from the study. She glanced around looking for any signs of who might be there. Her father hadn't mentioned having company first thing. She walked over to the study door and heard her name. Who is in there? She wondered. Why are they talking about me? She asked herself. Curiosity got the best of her. She lightly tapped on the door

"Come on in, Honey." David said to his daughter.

"Good morning Daddy." She said as she glanced over to the couch where an attractive young man she was guessing was about twenty-five was sitting. He was dressed in dark suit pants and a white button up shirt. She could see the outline of his muscles through the shirt. He looked as if he stayed in shape and she could tell he was definitely a businessman based on the way he kept his dark brown hair neat and trim.

Olivia smiled at the man and said. "Hello. I'm Olivia. David's daughter."

"Yes, I know." Was all he said with nothing more than a slight glance in her direction.

"David walked over to Olivia. Honey this is Avery Wentworth."

Olivia could tell that she had interrupted something important. "I'm sorry if I interrupted. I'll leave the two of you alone."

"No don't leave. This concerns you." David said.

"What do you mean?"

"Avery is the solution to your problem. He has agreed to marry you and raise your baby as his own. Nobody will be the wiser."

Olivia's head was spinning. She looked from Avery to her father and back to Avery. What was going on? "Wait! What?"

David knew that it would be a shock to her but it was the only way. He wasn't going to let a deadbeat dad into his family. Chris was not going to be a part of the Vandergate family. "I have taken care of everything. This will be an arranged marriage. You will both be well taken care of. I'll get you set up in a big house that is gated with full security. Nobody will come in unless it's announced first."

"But how is this supposed to work? This doesn't make sense." Olivia walked across the room to the mini bar and grabbed a bottle of water and started sipping at it.

"Simple." Her father said. "We are going to plan the biggest wedding you have ever seen. A month later we will announce the pregnancy and then when you go into labor we will announce that you had the baby early. Nobody will be the wiser. There is no time to waste though. Things must move quickly before you start showing."

Olivia had no idea what was going on but she knew that her father knew best. He seemed to have it all worked out. She would marry a complete stranger in order to give her child the life it deserved. "Whatever you think is best Daddy." She then turned to Avery. "And you are okay with all of this?"

Avery smiled. "Yes. Your father and I have talked in depth about it and have worked out a really good life for us all."

"Okay then. Now what?" She looked at her father for answers.

"First thing is I show the two of you to your new house. Then you move in and start getting to know each other and feeling comfortable around each other. All while planning the wedding of the century. We will be taking a lot of photos for the newspapers so that the town will get used to seeing the two of you together. There are a few charity events coming up that you will attend together and get lots of photos for. I'll have a schedule created for you to go by."

Everything was happening so fast that Olivia didn't really know what to say. She knew this was the best thing for her and her child but she didn't really understand what Avery could be running from. Why would he give up his entire life to pretend to love her? It didn't make sense to her.

"Okay just wait a minute. Hold on." Olivia felt like she was in some alter universe. "And you are good with all of this?" She asked Avery. She was pacing back and forth now. She ran her hands through her hair. "This is crazy."

Avery walked over to her. "Just calm down and think about this. This really is the best solution for everyone involved."

Olivia had no idea what was going on but she knew she really didn't have much of a choice. She almost whispered. "Okay."

Avery stood up and walked over to Olivia. "Your father has given me the keys to our new house and the directions. Would you like to go see it now?

"Yes of course." Olivia turned to her father and kissed him on the cheek. "I'll talk to you later Daddy."

Olivia and Avery walked to his black full size four wheel drive Chevy truck that was sitting outside in the drive. The ride over to their new house was pretty quiet. Olivia sat there staring out the window trying not to cry. She thought about everything that had happened over the past couple of days. My life is a mess. She thought to herself.

They drove up to a long driveway as her father said it was preceded by a gate with a security guard. They pulled up and the guard immediately opened the gate for them. As Avery drove through, he gave the guard a quick wave of his hand. The long-paved driveway was lined with beautiful pink and white dog wood trees. They stopped in front of a big two-story house that was eggshell white with a wraparound porch.

Olivia got out of the truck and walked over to the front door of her new house and waited for Avery to come and unlock it. When the door was unlocked, she walked in and looked around. She could see that her father thought of everything. It was fully furnished. She walked into the kitchen and opened the refrigerator and cabinets to find them fully stocked. She could literally step right into a new life with ease. All she needed was to get her clothes and things from her father's house. She walked up the stairs to explore the rest of the house stopping in front of the master bedroom not wanting to go in.

Avery walked up behind her. "It's okay I'll take the spare room at the end of the hall."

Olivia let out a big breath that she hadn't even realized she was holding. She walked into the room and took a quick look around. It was perfect. Her father truly had thought of everything.

Olivia walked down the hall to find Avery. She wasn't sure exactly what to say to him. It was strange living with a man that she didn't even know and planning a life with him. She stopped at the door. "Would you like some lunch. I can make us something and then maybe we can talk a little bit."

"Sure." Avery said.

Olivia went to the kitchen to see what her options were. She thought maybe something fast and easy. She got out the turkey, cheese, lettuce, tomato, and mayo then started making a sandwich. Then it dawned on her that she didn't know what Avery liked on his sandwiches. Maybe he didn't like mayo. She stood there at the counter holding the knife and looking at the jar of mayo.

Avery walked in and smiled. He knew exactly what she was thinking. "Mayo is fine."

Olivia let out a little laugh. "I guess it's going to take me a while to get to know you."

Avery picked up the sandwich and walked to the table to sit. "Yes and I really know nothing about you either. When your father called me last night, I admit it did take me a bit by surprise."

Olivia poured them both a glass of ice tea, sat it down on the table, and then grabbed her sandwich. She sat down across from Avery. "Why are you doing this? Why are you going to marry somebody you don't even know and raise a child that isn't yours? I get it that my father is probably paying you a lot of money but why do it?"

Avery knew that was a good question and deserved an answer. He wasn't sure he wanted to share his whole life story with her just yet but he did owe her the short version. "Well, I don't really have any family. My parents both died in an accident when I was young, I was raised by my grandmother, but she's very ill. She needs constant care, so I put her in a facility that can do what I can't. I visit as much as I can. We were very close but she doesn't remember much anymore. I've worked for your father for the past five years. It's a good fit. I have no family. He has offered me enough money where I'm set for life and I get a wife and child. I'm not stupid. I know it will take time for us to get to know each other and form a bond but who knows it may turn into actual love one day if we are open to it and give it a chance. Arranged marriages have been going on for an eternity so it's not like we are doing something completely unheard of."

Olivia hadn't thought about it that way. She did find it odd at first but it could work. It's not the craziest idea she had ever heard of.

Avery snapped Olivia out of her thoughts. "What about you? What's your story? Where is the father of your child?"

Olivia was almost teary eyed when she looked at Avery. "Oh you know the story. High school sweethearts. He was the school's star quarter back. We had dated all through high school and went to the same college. The only thing is; he decided not to grow up. Every night was the same thing. Party at the frat house, talk about the old high school days, plan the next party. It never changed. Chris and all of his good buddies enrolled in the bare minimum available classes and hoped that their dreams of playing pro football would come true with no backup plan in place. The day I found out I was pregnant I went to tell Chris and I found him passed out drunk from the party before. So, I wrote a Dear John letter and ran home to my father. I knew I couldn't raise a child like that. A child needs a life and what could Chris offer our child when his dreams of pro ball didn't work out. He had no idea what he wanted to be when he grew up." She couldn't help but cry. It seemed that it was all she did anymore. Crying made her angry. "I'm not going to do this." She said as she picked up the napkin and wiped the tears away. "I'm not going to sit here feeling sorry for myself."

Olivia hoped he didn't feel sorry for her, but that sounded pretty pathetic to even her own ears.

As she put the turkey away and cleaned up the mess, she glanced up at Avery. "I'm going to go to my father's and pack up some of my things. I will sit down with him and figure out how he wants us to handle everything."

"What do you mean?" Avery asked a bit confused.

"Well I just left Chris last night. I really don't think the town is going to believe that today I've already moved on and suddenly fell in love with you and moved in together. I'm sure my father will have an idea. So do you want to go with me?"

"Sure. Let's go."

Olivia's mind was swirling with thoughts and ideas as she sat in the truck. She had a few ideas that might work. She wanted to run them by her father. She barely noticed the music playing in the background. One of her favorite country songs was playing. Olivia laughed a little. "You know when I was in high school, I thought country was horrible. I was rock and roll all the way. Give me some Bon Jovi, Poison, Def Leppard any day. I loved the hair bands as they were called. Look at me now. Now all I listen to is country music."

Avery laughed. "That's a good thing. You have crossed over to the good side. The country side."

When they got to her father's house they walked right to the study where she knew he would be.

David got up and greeted his daughter. "How was the house?"

"It was great Daddy. I love it. We even had a sandwich before coming back over."

"That's great. What's up though? I can tell when you have something on your mind." He said with a smile.

Olivia walked over to the couch with Avery following behind. She sat down and began to fidget with her sweater. "Well Daddy. I left Chris last night. I don't think it will be believable for Avery and me to go to town holding hands and start this big show of affection. How will people believe that I broke up with Chris last night and then today I have a new man?"

David poured himself a drink and slowly sipped it as he pondered the question. "Okay that is a good question. What did you have in mind?"

Olivia stood up and began pacing. "I've been thinking about it. What if Avery and I go on a vacation somewhere for a few weeks? I buy some post cards and send back here to a few select people explaining how Chris and I broke up and I needed a break. And I just happened to run into Avery who is there on business for you. People will believe we aren't strangers because he's worked for you for years and they have probably seen the two of you together at some point. Things start moving along. I keep these few busy bodies in the loop full well knowing they will spread the gossip like wild fires. And then when we get back from vacation it's already in everyone's head that we are a couple then we start all your events. It's still happening a little fast but might go over a little better than overnight we fell in love. What do you two think?"

Avery spoke first. "That's actually a really good idea. And it will give us some alone time to start getting comfortable around each other before we go out in public. Nobody is going to believe we love each other if we are awkward around each other. One question though. You haven't mentioned any friends. Don't you have close friends who can help make this all look real?"

Olivia thought about it for a minute and couldn't think of many names. "Not really. I have friends if you can call them that. I have people I hang out with but they are all pretty superficial. They are my friend because of Daddy's money and the things they can get from me. I can't think if one person who actually cares about me other than Andrea and she's out of town right now." Her eyes had a sadness about them.

"Who is Andrea?" Avery asked.

Olivia snapped out of her sadness for a moment. "Oh you will like her. She's great. We've been friends since kindergarten but life has gotten in the way and we haven't had much time to spend with each other lately."

David hadn't even thought about some of the things they were saying. He knew it all made sense. He interrupted her trip down memory lane. "Yes, I agree. It's settled. You will leave tonight for a long vacation."

Olivia started to say something when she was interrupted by her cell phone ringing. As she looked down, she gasped. "Oh no. It's Chris. What do I do?"

"You stand tough. Tell him it's over." Her father said sternly.

Olivia's hands were somewhat shaky as she answered the phone. "Hello"

"Olivia what is going on?" She heard Chris say.

"Chris I told you everything I had to say in the letter. I'm not coming back to school. I'm going to get on the job training from

Daddy. I don't need a degree to work for him"

"Olivia, you can't just leave me after all these years and for no reason."

"Chris there was plenty of reason. All you do is party all the time. I've grown up. I've outgrown you. It's over." She hung up the phone fearing she would say too much. Tears were building up in her eyes. Her heart was breaking inside. She loved Chris and had loved him for years. Having that conversation was one of the hardest things she had ever done. "I'm going to go pack." She said to her father and Avery.

Chapter Three

As Olivia boarded the plane on her way to Hawaii with a man that wasn't a complete stranger but wasn't somebody she knew well. She wondered where she went wrong in life. She walked down the aisle and put her carry on in the overhead compartment. She always felt a little sick when it came to airplanes.

Avery could tell that she looked nervous. "Are you okay?"

"Fine. I will be glad when we are landing. I'm not fond of plane rides." She said as she gripped the arm rest of her seat.

"We'll be there in no time." He said trying to reassure her.

Olivia lay back in her seat and drifted off to sleep. She was exhausted from all the stress of the night before. As she lay there thoughts of Chris filled her mind. Her head knew that she made the right decision but her heart was shattered at the moment. She tossed and turned in her seat restlessly. Before she knew it Avery was waking her up. They had made it to the airport already. Her father had called ahead to have a car waiting for them.

Olivia stepped off the plane and walked to the car with Avery beside her neither really saying much. It was a bit of an awkward situation but they had both made up their own minds and were going to move forward with their decision.

When they got to the hotel Olivia said "I have a reservation for Vandergate. There should be two rooms."

The woman looked at her computer and said. "I'm only showing one room. A suite with a hot tub."

Olivia couldn't believe her father only booked them one room but figured if they were going to be married, she might as well get used to sharing a room with him. "That's fine. My mistake." She said as she signed the paper and picked up the room card.

Avery picked up their bags and followed behind her not really sure of what to say.

Olivia opened the door to the hotel and then turned to Avery. "Here is your home for the next two weeks."

Avery smiled and walked in. "It's perfect. What do you want to do? We can go site seeing and pick up some of those post cards you mentioned or stay in."

Olivia was going to make the best of that vacation. She was in Hawaii with a handsome man who by the way was about to be her husband. She needed to get used to the idea of spending time with him. "Let's go site seeing."

They spent the next few hours going from place to place taking it all in. It was extremely pretty on the island. She stopped off at a tourist stand and picked up several post cards with the word Hawaii on the front and a picture of the water. Then they walked the beaches for a while before going to one of the bars for a drink.

Avery asked. "What do you want to drink?"

"Something non-alcoholic. Maybe some kind of fruity drink with a big umbrella." She said with a giggle.

Avery told the bartender to surprise her as long as there wasn't any alcohol it in it would be perfect. They sat there for a few hours taking in the scenery and making small talk.

Avery sipped his drink as he looked across the table at Olivia. "What about your mother where is she?"

Sadness fell over her. "My mother died when I was twelve. She had breast cancer. She fought it for years but it kept coming back until finally she had no more fight in her."

"I'm sorry. I shouldn't have asked."

Olivia waved him off. "No. Don't worry about it. If we are going to be married asking about my mother seems reasonable." She smiled.

Avery laughed. "I guess you're right. I am going to be your husband and all."

"Well, I certainly could have done worse." She laughed before taking a sip of her drink.

After they talked for while they walked back to the hotel.

Olivia walked into the room first and kicked off her shoes. "I'm going to go soak in a hot bath if you don't mind."

"Sure, no problem. I'm going to order some room service. Do you want anything?"

"Yes please. Order me anything. I'm a little hungry." She smiled.

She walked into the bathroom to draw a bath. Her feet hurt from all the walking but she had enjoyed herself. Avery isn't that bad she thought to herself. She sank down in the tub and let the bubbles flow across her skin. She got out when she heard the knock at the door. She assumed it was their food. She quickly dried off and wrapped herself in a robe. Her hair was kind of mess but she didn't think he would mind.

When she walked into the living room area of the suite she saw Avery setting up dinner. He had ordered steak, baked potatoes and a salad. She saw a couple of bottles of water and juice.

Avery saw her walk in. "Dinner is served."

"It smells delicious. I didn't realize I was as hungry as I am." She said as she walked over to the table. She sat down and started eating. She cut into her well-done steak. "This is cooked to perfection."

"Uh no. That is burnt. This is cooked to perfection." He smiled as he cut into his medium well steak that was still a little pink inside.

"Oh no that is disgusting." She laughed as she turned away like it was really grossing her out.

They both ate their food neither really saying much. They were both still finding their way in the relationship. It had only been a day but they were falling right into a routine.

After dinner Olivia got out the post cards that she bought in town. She knew exactly who to send them to and what to say that would do exactly what she needed done. The first one she addressed to the nosy Mrs. Peterson.

Dear Mrs. Peterson,

I'm so very sorry that I can't make it to the charity ball planning meeting next week. I'm out of town right now and won't be back in time to make it. I recently broke up with my longtime boyfriend, Chris. I needed some time to get a way. I'm sorry. I'm sure you are too busy to hear all my drama. I'll be back in a few weeks and then we can get to planning.

C'ya soon

Olivia

One down a couple more to go. The second one would go to the lovely little busy body, Mrs. Anderson.

Dear Mrs. Anderson,

I wanted to let you know that I'm out of town for a few days. I have recently gone through a sad break up from Chris. I don't want to trouble you with my problems. I'm fine now. I'm on vacation and enjoying myself. I wanted to write to you and let you know that the charity auction will go on as planned and I will be back in a couple weeks to get started on the planning for it.

I'll talk to you soon,

Olivia

Olivia looked at Avery. "Ok those are the two nosiest women in the town. By the time we get back everyone in town will know that I am no longer with Chris. Next thing is for me to send a couple texts to friends who will put the word around about the break up."

She grabbed her phone and texted her friend Andrea.

Hey Andrea. It's me. Guess what I'm in Hawaii. I know I know. I'll call you later. Long story short. I broke up with Chris and needed to get away for a while.

She sat her phone down and looked back at Avery. "When we get back I will go to these charity planning meetings and if you like you can come with me and we can get people used to seeing us together. Then we will do the actual events as a couple. What do you think?"

Avery was amazed at how much thought she had put into it all. "I think this is going to work perfectly. I'm beat. I'm going to go ahead and call it a night. I'll sleep out here on the sofa."

"Okay. Yeah, I'm tired too. It was a long day. I'll see you in the morning." Olivia turned and walked to the bedroom. She felt a little bad about making him sleep on the sofa but she wasn't quite ready to share her bed even if he was her future husband. She crawled in the bed and snuggled under the big blue blanket. It wasn't long before she was a sleep.

The next morning Olivia woke to the smell of bacon and eggs. She assumed Avery had ordered room service, which normally would have been good but not today. She jumped up out of bed and ran to the bathroom. She made it just in time. After getting sick for what seemed like forever, she got up and walked over to the sink. She rinsed her mouth, brushed her teeth, and then felt the need to rinse her mouth again. She looked in the mirror and could see that her face was pale and her hair was all over the place. *God, I hope this entire pregnancy isn't going to be like this.* She said to herself.

Avery tapped on the bathroom door. "Is everything okay in there?"

Olivia looked over at the door but not quite ready to move. "Yes. I'm fine. I'll be right out but can you do me a favor first?"

"Of course. Anything." Avery said.

"Can you please get rid of the eggs?"

Avery couldn't help but laugh. "Sure." He said as he dumped them in the trash.

Olivia finally came out of the bathroom and poured herself a glass of water. She picked up a piece of dry toast and ate it hoping it would settle her stomach. "I'm sorry about the eggs." She said to Avery.

"Don't be. It's not a problem. What do you want to do today?"

Olivia hadn't really put much thought into this vacation if you could call it that. She was really planning on hiding out not so much taking a vacation, but she knew that wasn't fair to Avery. "I don't know. You pick."

Avery thought about it for a few minutes. "How about we charter a boat and take a tour around the island of Hawaii? I've actually never been here before. Is your stomach up for that?"

"Yeah, it sounds like fun. I think I'll be fine now."

They called down to the front desk and got it all set up. It should be a good day for a boat ride. The weather was great. It didn't take them long to get to the front desk to meet the driver taking them to the boat. Olivia's stomach settled as they drove to the dock. They got on the boat with no troubles and headed out onto the ocean.

Olivia leaned back against the seat on the boat and let the breeze flow through her hair. The charter company packed a lunch for them included in their cost. After a few hours out there, Olivia was starting to get hungry. She got out the cooler and handed Avery his lunch. The company had packed them sandwiches, sodas, fruit and chips. It was a good lunch especially since Olivia hadn't felt much like eating breakfast that morning. They spent a few more hours out there before heading back to shore. It was a long day but it was well worth it. They both had the time of their lives. Olivia took lots of photos for her scrap book to show everyone in town. She had to make sure their story was believable. When they got back to the hotel, she was completely tired out.

They walked back up to their room and Olivia was tired but didn't want to ignore Avery. It was too hard to talk on the boat all day. It was too loud. With everything happening so fast they haven't really talked much at all.

Olivia walked in the room first and kicked off her shoes. "I think I'm going to take a quick shower. Do you want to watch a movie when I get out?"

"Yeah. That's sounds great. I'll throw some popcorn in the microwave. I saw some over in the kitchen area." Avery said as he went to get it started.

"Great. I'll be right out."

Olivia jumped in the shower to wash up real quick. She wouldn't have minded soaking in a hot tub but was afraid she would fall asleep. Being on the boat all day was exhausting. She got out, dressed and went to find Avery in the living room.

"What do you want to see? Romance? Action Adventure?"

"You pick." She said.

"Okay. Well, I'm a guy." He said with a laugh. "So, I'm thinking action adventure."

Olivia laughed. "Okay. Sounds good."

They sat on the couch and started the movie. The opening credits hadn't finished before Olivia rested her head in Avery's lap, and fell asleep.

Avery grabbed a small throw that she had lying on the back of the couch and covered her up as she lay on him. He thought it was kind of nice. He sat there for the next couple of hours watching tv not wanting to disturb her. When the movie went off, he thought he should probably move before his legs fell off. He scooted out from under her and then gently picked her up and carried her to her bed. After tucking her all in he went back to the couch.

The next morning Olivia woke up in the bed and looked around a little confused. She rubbed her eyes and ran her fingers through her hair. She got up out of bed and slipped her feet into the slippers she had by the bed and walked into the other room. She saw Avery reading the newspaper. "Good morning."

Avery looked up from the paper. "Good morning. Did you sleep well?"

Yawning Olivia said. "Yes. I did actually. Thanks for getting me to bed. I was exhausted."

"Yeah. You didn't watch much of the movie." He laughed. "Would you like some breakfast?"

Olivia put her hand to her stomach feeling a little sick. "I think I'll wait a bit for food."

Avery understood. "What's on our agenda for the day?" He asked.

Olivia let out a small breath and then walked over to get a bottle of water. "You know. I don't really know. I really didn't put much thought into this trip. We have already gone site seeing, and chartered a boat and watched tv and we still have a lot of vacation left." She walked over to the table where the hotel left a stack of tourist attraction books for them and started thumbing through them.

"How about we talk for a little bit? We really don't know much about each other." Avery said.

"Okay. That's true. What do you want to know?"

"For starters how far along are you?"

"I haven't been to the doctor yet and will do that as soon as I get home, but I can't be farther than two months right now. So, it will be easy for us to go with Daddy's plan of just saying I went into premature labor."

"Yes, I agree. First thing; you need to go to the doctor but maybe we could do that while we are here too. Just so we get our facts straight. We don't want the busy bodies to spread rumors the moment you go see them."

Olivia's face dropped. "I hadn't even thought about that. Yes. Let's do that. Let's get a doctor appointment here. Find out exactly what my due date is and how far along I am and make sure the baby is fine. Then when we get back home, I'll find a doctor in the next town over that way nobody will see me coming or going to my visits."

"Do you think all that is necessary?" Avery asked. "You might be going a tad overboard."

"I'm just trying to be extra careful."

"I understand." He said. "I'm just thinking that once they see us together it wouldn't hurt for people to see you coming and going from the doctor. It might actually help the story."

She sat there for a minute before talking letting it all sink in. "You know. You might be right. Of course, the first thing some people will say is that we are only together because of the baby." She laughed. "Well, that wouldn't be a lie now, would it?"

Avery couldn't help but laugh too. He shook his head. "Go ahead and see if you can get an appointment."

Olivia called down to the front desk to have them get her an appointment for as soon as possible. They said they would call her later with one which they did. She was able to get one for after lunch that day. It helped being able to use her father's name or money to get things done a little faster.

"Okay we can see the doctor after lunch."

"That was fast. Do you want me to come with you?"

Olivia smiled. "Of course. This is your child now. I want you at every appointment."

"Okay then. Why don't we go get a late breakfast and pick up a few things from town and then head over to the doctor?"

"Sounds good."

They left the hotel room and walked to the closest diner. They sat at a booth and started looking over the menu.

"I don't know what I want." Olivia said. "My eyes want one thing but I know my stomach won't want me to get that."

Avery tried not to laugh "I do feel bad for you having morning sickness so early into the pregnancy. I really do. Try something kind of bland like oatmeal."   "No thank you." Olivia laughed. "I have never liked oatmeal. I think I'll go with the French toast. That shouldn't be too bad on me."

The waitress came over and they placed their orders. As they sat there waiting, Olivia thought about how It had only been a couple of days of them being together but they were fairly comfortable around each other. They were like old friends. The love wasn't there yet but Olivia had hopes that it would come. She was happy that they at least liked each other.

Chapter Four

Olivia walked into the doctor's office with Avery close behind. She walked up to the desk and gave them her name then they sat down and waited to be called. It was only moment before she was called.

Olivia got up to go in and turned to Avery. "Are you coming?"

Avery stood up rubbing his sweaty palms on his jeans. "Why am I so nervous?" He said as he followed her into the room.

The doctor was holding her chart. "Hello Olivia. I'm Dr. Smart. I know I know. I've heard it all before." The doctor laughed.

Olivia smiled.

"So, you are here today to confirm your pregnancy. Correct?"

"Yes." Olivia said. "I've taken three home tests and they all said positive."

"Three?" The doctor questioned.

"Well, this was a little unplanned and I didn't quite believe the tests."

The doctor gave her a reassuring smile. "Okay I'm going to ask you some questions, have you give me a urine sample, and then we will listen for a heat beat and next do some measurements. I should be able to give you an accurate due date by the time we are done."

Olivia's head was spinning. Everything was happening so fast. She went in the other room and gave her urine sample and the nurse did their own pregnancy test to confirm what she already knew. She was pregnant. Then everything happened as the doctor said.

Dr. Smart said "Okay now would you like to hear your baby's heartbeat?"

"Yes!" Olivia immediately said.

"Okay. Let's get started." She rolled the handle around Olivia's stomach until the sound started. "There it is."

Olivia started crying. "That's amazing." She looked over at Avery who had a look of Awe on his face.

"I've never heard anything like it before." Avery said.

"When can I see the baby? When do I get an ultra sound?"

"That comes a bit later. It's still a little early for that. You need to make an appointment with a doctor when you get back home and they might do one on your first visit with them since you will be further along but it will be up to that doctor. I'm setting your due date at December fifteenth and I'm going to go ahead and give you some prenatal vitamins to get you started until you see your doctor."

"Thank you, Doctor.," Olivia said as they were walking out of the office.

As they walked out of the office Avery asked Olivia. "Do you want me to get a cab or do you want to walk?"

"Let's walk. It's a nice day out." Olivia without even knowing it let her hand fall to her stomach.

"It's amazing, isn't it?" Avery said.

Olivia snapped out of her thoughts for a minute. "Yes, it is. Am I doing the right thing by not telling Chris?"

"I think you are if he is like you say he is. A child needs a stable life not a father who wants to party all the time and not grow up. You can't put a child to bed and have its father in the other room jumping up and down shouting with his friends about the great game on tv. That's not a life for a child. I will be a hands on there for him or her father."

Olivia liked the sounds of that. They walked back to the hotel not saying much just taking in the scenery.

Days went by of the same old same old. Get up go to town, go out to eat. Olivia was getting a little bored with it all. She picked up the phone to call her father.

"Daddy. I've missed you."

"How's it going Honey? How is Avery treating you?"

"Avery is great, Daddy. I saw a doctor while I was here just for a checkup and to see how far along I am. Everything is fine with the baby and my due date is December 15th."

"That's perfect. We have plenty of time to get things in order. How much longer are you going to be gone?"

"Well, that's what I wanted to ask you. I'm getting kind of bored and would like to get home to my new house and my new life. Do you think we have been gone long enough?"

"I think so. Your post cards did the trick. It was all over town the day they arrived that Chris is out of the picture. And your texts to your friends about Avery spread the word that there is a new guy. You can go to all the event plannings with Avery and the events with him without any worry. Everything will be perfect."

Olivia hung up the phone filled with excitement. She was ready to get home. She hated all this hiding out stuff, but knew it had to be done to protect her child. Olivia went to find Avery to tell him the good news.

"Avery!" She said with a little more excitement than expected. "Daddy says we can come home. The post cards and texts have done their jobs."

Avery had mixed feelings about going home. He wasn't completely sure what he was supposed to do when he got back. Was he supposed to go to work or stay home with Olivia? He had a lot to figure out. "That's great. I'll book us a flight for the first available one out tomorrow."

"I can't wait to get back to our new house." Olivia said. "We didn't even get a chance to really check it all out. Everything was so rushed." She was filled with excitement. She ran over and kissed Avery on the lips very quickly and then ran off to start packing.

Avery stood there for a minute "What just happened?" He said quietly to the empty room. "She's just excited. It didn't mean anything."

They both went to bed early so they could get up and make the early flight. It was time to go home.

Chapter Five

Olivia was happy to be pulling into the drive of her new house. It was private and the limo had tented windows so nobody would see that Avery was coming home with her. She knew they had a few holes in their story. Avery couldn't move right in. He was going to have to stay somewhere else for a few months while they pretend to be dating. After the engagement was set, he would be able to move in.

She walked in and looked around before going upstairs to pick out the room she wanted for the nursery. "Avery. I would like to make this room here the nursery. What do you think?"

Avery nodded. "Yes, that makes sense. It's the closest one to the master bedroom."

"I know it's way too early yet but I can't wait until I can start fixing this room up."

Avery didn't want to kill the mood but he had some questions. "I think we need to go see your father now that we are back. We still have a lot to figure out. Like what I'm supposed to do. Am I to continue working with him and do my nine to five job or what?"

Olivia hadn't thought about any of that. "You're right. Let's go see Daddy."

David was more than excited to see his daughter back. He ran up and threw his arms around her instantly. "I'm glad you're home."

"Me too Daddy. We have some questions about everything. We're still working out the details on all of this."

"Okay. Lay them on me. I've been doing a lot of thinking while you were gone."

Olivia was all business. "Okay. What about Avery? Does he just go to work at the company as before? Do his normal work? Doesn't he need to stay at his apartment for a while too? We can't have some strange guy move in with me a couple of weeks after a break up and expect it to be believable."

David listened carefully to his daughter's concerns. "Yes, that all sounds good. Avery continues to work for me as always and I agree you should probably keep your apartment until we make the wedding announcement. People will think things moved quickly but they will see how happy you are and overlook it."

They had a plan in motion. Avery would go to work every day. In the evenings they would start going on dates to dinner and things publicly so people would start seeing them together holding hands and things. It would all be subtle but it would be effective.

The days went by without a hitch. Olivia went to meet Mrs. Peterson to do some final planning for the charity ball that would be put on by her father's company.

"Hello Mrs. Peterson. Everything looks wonderful. I believe it's going to be a successful night and we should raise a lot of money for charity."

Mrs. Peterson smiled. "I think so Dear. Now tell me about this handsome young man you have been seen with lately. You two seem joined at the hip."

Olivia blushed a little. "Mrs. Peterson." She said with a smile. "That's Avery and he is so perfect for me. We've only been together for a short time but you know how when you just know you just know. I think he's the one for me."

Mrs. Peterson gave her a tap on the shoulder. "Mr. Peterson and I only dated two weeks before we got married and we were together for fifty years before he passed away. You're right sometimes you just know."

Olivia finished up with the final details for the event. Everything was right on track for it to take place next week. She left and went straight home to catch up with Avery who was supposed to meet her there.

When Olivia walked in, she could see something was wrong. Avery looked upset like he had been crying and he was setting his cell phone down as she walked in. She ran over to him. "Avery is everything okay? What happened?"

Avery wiped at his eyes. "That was the nursing home. My grandmother passed away."

Olivia put her hand to her mouth. Then quickly ran to him. She put her arms around him and held him. She wanted to take his pain away. She knew too well what he must be going through. The pain she felt when she lost her mother was almost unbearable. She would do anything to take his pain away but knew she couldn't. Being there for him was all she could do.

He pulled away just enough to lean down and kiss her gently on the lips. She didn't back away. He pulled her in closer as he kissed her. The kiss lingered on for what seemed like an eternity.

Olivia felt a shiver go up her spine. What was she doing? She put her hands under his shirt and started to remove it and tossed it on the floor.

Avery scooped her up in his arms and carried her to the living room. He gently laid her on the couch. As he ran her fingers through her hair, he kissed every inch of her body. He made soft passionate love to her.

Olivia wrapped Avery's arms around her as they lay there on the couch sleeping. She didn't know what had just happened. Had they finally came out of the friend zone or was he upset about his grandmother that he didn't really know what was happening.

A few hours went by and Avery jumped up. "Oh no! I shouldn't have fallen asleep. I have to get to the nursing home and make arrangements for my grandma. What was I thinking?" He started scrambling around for his shirt and keys.

"It's okay Avery. I can go with you if you want."

Avery looked over at her realizing what just happened and feeling bad about being so insensitive about it. "Oh, I'm so sorry Olivia. I didn't mean to do that and then jump up and leave. That's not how I wanted our first time together to be. I'm so sorry."

Olivia wrapped herself in the blanket that was on the back of the couch. "It's okay. I understand. Let me throw some clothes on and I'll go with you. You don't have to handle this all alone."

She went into the bathroom and quickly got dressed. She tossed her hair up in a ponytail to get it out of her face and then they left to make arrangements.

Avery was her only family so he didn't plan anything big. He had her cremated and he planned to scatter her ashes at her favorite spot. It was something that he and Olivia would do together.

The days went by with sadness in Avery's heart but he got through it the best he could. It was the night of the charity ball and Olivia was dressed in a beige floor length gown. Her hair was left long with a few curls in it.

Avery picked her up in one of her father's limos and they walked into the ball arm in arm. All eyes were on them as they walked in. The town people expected them to come together as they have been seen together almost nightly since they got back from vacation and their emotions didn't have to be faked. They were truly in love and had been through a lot already.

Avery turned to Olivia. "May I have this dance."

She smiled. "Of course."

He held her close to his chest as they slow danced. It was as if they were the only two in the room. He leaned down to whisper in her ear. "I love you."

"I love you too." She said.

Olivia made her rounds around the room talking to all the guests and plugging the charity hoping to get a successful turnout on donations. By the end of the night her feet were killing her. She should have rethought the high heels for the evening. When her and Avery got into the limo to leave, she kicked off her shoes. "That is so much better."

Avery reached down for her feet and turned her around in the seat so she was all stretched out and comfortable. He started massaging her sore tired feet.

"Oh my God that feels great. You can do that all night if you want." She said with a laugh.

When they got back to her house, he walked her to the door and was going to leave.

"You don't have to go. Go ahead and come in. Let's plan the wedding."

Avery laughed. "Shouldn't I ask you first?"

Olivia laughed. "Well, we haven't really done anything by the books in this relationship now have we?"

"That's very true. Let's get started."

Olivia walked over to the kitchen table where she had everything laid out. "Okay we need to do it before I start showing too much. So, I was thinking how about not this weekend but next weekend?"

"You want to plan your entire wedding in two weeks?"
"It's not that big of a deal." She said. "With Daddy's connections. A couple of phone calls and it's all set. He will call the country club tomorrow and reserve it for the reception. I will get a dress at the bridal store tomorrow or I'll call a designer. Not really sure yet. You can pick up a tuxedo at the mall if you don't have one already. Catering we have plenty of time to give notice to them. So yeah, really, we can get it all done by then. I will drop off a guest list to the invitation store. They will print them and mail them all within a couple of days.

That gives our guests almost two weeks' notice. That's plenty of time."

Avery knew the day was coming but now it's really here. He didn't mind because he had truly fallen in love with Olivia and he knew she felt the same about him. "Sounds great. I can't wait to be married to you."

"Okay then it's settled."

Avery got up to leave. "It's late I think I better go home." He walked over and gave Olivia a long kiss goodnight. "I'll see you tomorrow.

Olivia was exhausted from the charity ball but she was too excited to sleep. She was going to be married in two short weeks. She had a busy day ahead of her tomorrow. She went to bed to try and rest.

When she got up the next day, she felt horrible. She ran to the bathroom and made it just in time to get sick in the toilet instead of the bedroom floor. She looked in the mirror but didn't like what she saw looking back. She started the shower hoping that maybe it would help make her feel better. When she finished up, she went to get her day started. It was going to be a long day but it was going to be fun. She couldn't wait to get started planning her wedding.

First, she called her best friend Andrea and asked her to be her maid of honor. She accepted without hesitation and agreed to go shopping with her. The two of them spent the entire day bouncing from place to place getting everything on the list all taken care of. Olivia was excited to tell Avery later how much she got accomplished in just one day.

Everything was moving along with ease as Olivia thought it would. Her father's name and money helped it all get done.

Chapter Six

The wedding day had arrived. Olivia was nervous and excited all in one. She loved Avery and couldn't wait to walk down that aisle to start the next chapter of her life with him.

She was dressed in a floor length white Vera Wang wedding dress with the traditional six-foot train. Her hair was in an up do with a white headband trimmed in pink roses.

Avery stood at the front of the church awaiting his bride to be as the music started to fill the room. The flower child and ring bearer walked down the aisle. The little girl tossing pink rose petals left and right with the little boy trying to keep up. Next came the bride's maids wearing pink satin dresses and holding pink roses floral bouquets in one hand and using their other hand to wrap around the arm of the groomsmen walking beside her.

As the wedding march started everyone stood to await the bride's entrance. All eyes were on the door. The ushers opened the door and everyone's mouth dropped. The most beautiful bride in the world graced them with her presence at least that's what Avery thought. She walked down the aisle arm in arm with her father.

The preacher asked who give the bride away and David proudly said. "I do." Then he found his seat.

Olivia without hesitation said "I do."

Avery walked his bride out of the church and into the limo where they went onto the reception that neither really wanted to go to. They wanted to run off and have a private moment.

They went to the reception and were flooded with gifts. Olivia had the limo driver pack them all to the car for them. When they were finally able to leave, she was more than ready to get back home and relax. Her feet were throbbing.

The next few days went by with Olivia putting away all the wedding gifts and addressing thank you cards to send out to everyone. The town had accepted her and Avery with no problem. She went to check the mail and was shocked to see a card from Chris. Inside it said. "Congratulations on the wedding. I'm glad you found somebody to make you happy. You deserve that." Olivia couldn't help but get a little teary at it. She still felt a little bad at how everything went down but she loved Avery more than anything. It may not have started out the way a relationship normally would but she wouldn't trade it for the world.

Olivia spent the next few weeks trying to decide which theme she wanted in the nursery. She didn't know if she was having a boy or a girl yet. It was still too early so she thought she would go with a neutral theme like teddy bears and for colors maybe green, yellow and tan. She was in the nursery looking around when a sharp pain hit her like a knife. She doubled over onto the floor and that's when she saw the blood. She was scared to death and didn't know what to do. She grabbed her cell and called her father. "Meet me at the hospital." She sobbed. "I think I'm losing the baby." She yelled for one of the guards to come help her.

He came running, picked her up, and carried her to the car. He drove as fast as he could to the hospital and yelled for a doctor. A nurse came to her pulling a gurney. The driver helped get her up on it. The nurse and a couple orderlies wheeled her into an exam room.

After an hour or so the dr. came in. "I'm very sorry to tell you this Olivia but you have lost the baby."

Olivia burst into tear crying uncontrollably. "No! No! This can't be happening. Why?"

The doctor gave her a sedative to help relax her and then they called Avery who was on her chart as her husband and told him what had happened.

Avery got to the hospital as fast as he could. He was upset and trying to hold back tears. That was as much his child as hers. He had come to think of it like that anyway. He ran to her side but found her still sleeping. He pulled up a chair and sat there for hours watching over her as she slept.

Olivia's eyes started to flutter as she opened them, she saw Avery sitting in a chair. She started crying all over again. "I lost the baby." She said in between sobs.

Avery went to her side, leaned down and put his arms around her. "I'm so sorry." He held her tight for a few minutes. "We'll get through this together."

She pulled away. "Find a doctor please and see when I can go home. I don't want to stay here any longer than I have to."

Avery did as she asked. He went to find a doctor.

It was only a few hours later when they were able to leave. Olivia had let her driver leave so she rode home with Avery. Neither said a word on the ride. When they got home Avery helped her to the bedroom and helped her in bed.

"You rest." He said to her as he kissed her on the forehead. "Let me know if you need anything."

Olivia started crying all over again.

Avery put his arms around her and held her close until she fell asleep. Then he laid her down and gently covered her up.

Olivia slept through the night and got up early the next morning. She jumped in the shower and left before Avery got up. She didn't want to see him. She went to her father's house.

David put his arms around his daughter as she cried into his chest. "It's okay Honey. It will be alright. Where's Avery?"

The waterworks came flooding. "He's at home. I left while he was still sleeping. I don't know what to do Daddy. I love him, but he only married me because of the deal you made him. Now that I've lost the baby there is no reason for him to stay. What am I going to do?" She went to the couch and put her head down and cried for minutes.

"Honey. Avery loves you. It might have begun unconventional but that man loves you."

"I'm going to stay here for a few days to think. Please don't let him know I'm here."

"Of course, Honey but I think you are making the wrong decision."

Olivia went to her old bedroom and lay down on the bed. All she could seem to do was cry. She hugged her pillow and let the tears come down until her pillow was completely wet. Then she flipped it over and began soaking that side. She knew she would have to talk to Avery at some point but she didn't want to do it right now. She needed some time alone.

Avery paced back and forth in the quiet house. He had called Olivia's cell phone a dozen times getting voicemail each time. He called David. If anyone knew where she was it would be him.

"David. It's Avery. Have you seen Olivia? I'm worried about her."

"Avery she just needs time. She's here and resting. I think she will probably stay here tonight."

"I'm coming over."

"No don't do that. She is upset and needs some time alone. She is feeling lost right now. She said the only reason you married her was because of our arrangement and now you have no reason to stay with her."

Avery almost dropped the phone. "I love her. Please tell her that I love her."

"I will. Just give her a few days. She will get through this."

Avery hung up the phone and broke down and cried. His whole life was turning upside down. His wife, the woman he loved, just lost their child and she was gone too. She didn't want to see him. What was he supposed to do now? His whole world was falling apart.

Days went by with no word from Olivia. He didn't know what he was supposed to do. She wouldn't see him or talk to him on the phone. David told him not to come to the house. He had to talk to her. He loved her.

The doorbell rang and he went to the door to get it. It was one of David's messengers with a big yellow envelope. He took it and thanked the man then turned and walked inside.

When he opened it, he saw a check for five million dollars and annulment papers. There was a note from Olivia also.

Dear Avery,

I'm so sorry that things happened the way they did. Without the baby you have no reason to stay with me. You can keep the house and my father has provided for you. All I need you to do is sign the papers and you are free to go on with your life with no hassles from me. I wish you all the best in your life.

Always

Olivia

Avery dropped to the floor. She couldn't do this to him. This couldn't be happening. He wasn't in it for the money or the baby. He loved her and didn't want to live his life without her. He cried for a while before getting angry. He wouldn't let her give up on them. He tried to call her but she wouldn't answer. He left message after message on her voicemail but nothing worked. She wouldn't call him back.

Days had gone by and he hadn't shaved or showed. He had lost everything and had no will to go on. He read the note over and over to the point that it was ripped and worn in places. It was starting to fade. He couldn't stop reading it. Finally, something clicked. "I'll get her back." He said aloud. He jumped up and went to take a shower. He shaved and made himself presentable. He had to try and win her back. He grabbed the check and the papers and went to David's.

When he got to the front gate, he asked the guard to let him speak to David. "David please let me in. I have to talk to her. If after I talk to her, she still wants me to sign then I will sign the papers and get out of her life, but you owe me at least this."

David agreed and the gates opened for Avery to drive through.

Avery came in the house and found Olivia in the study alone. "Olivia, we need to talk."

Olivia began to cry. "There isn't anything to talk about. I'm giving you your life back."

"I don't have a life if you aren't in it. I love you. Yes, maybe we started out under different reasons, but that's not how it ended up. I love you and that's all there is to it. I want you not an annulment. Tell me you don't love me and I will sign the papers and leave."

Olivia wiped the tears away. "It's best for us both if we just end this."

"That's not what I asked you to say. Tell me you don't love me and I'll go."

Olivia sobbed. "I can't do that. I do love you. But love isn't enough. I've learned that the hard way."

"Our love is enough. We didn't plan this. We both had other plans, other loves but we were brought together for a reason. We make each other whole. We belong together and we will make it work. We're married and I want to keep it that way."

Olivia ran to him and put her arms around him. She loved him more than life itself.

The next few months were hard for Olivia. She had lost a baby. Even if she never got to hold that baby, she had bonded with it. She would never fully get over the loss but she would learn to deal with it the best she could.

Chapter Seven

It was late October and the town was getting ready for the fall festival. There would be a parade through the town the high school queen candidates throwing candy from the float as they strolled by. Kids lined up both sides of the street gathering candy in their buckets. Local venders with hot chocolate stands set up along the parade route. It was the town's tradition.

Olivia and Avery got ready and drove to town. As they were walking hand in hand never happier Olivia stopped dead in her tracks.

Avery looked down at her. "What is it?"

Olivia stammered. "It's…. It's Chris. He's over there. I haven't seen him since I broke up with him."

Avery looked in the direction she was looking but didn't know who she was looking at. "Do you want to leave?"

Olivia squeezed his hand. "No. I've made my decision and I'm more than happy with it. We can't avoid him. I think he saw me. So, we'll say hello."

They walked over to where Chris was standing. Olivia said. "Hi Chris. It's been a while. How have you been?"

Chris was a little taken aback. He hadn't seen her in a while. "Good. I'm good. How are you?"

It was awkward making small talk like that. "I'm good. This is my husband, Avery."

Avery held his hand out to shake hands. "It's nice meeting you."

Chris said the same and then they stood there for a minute nobody saying anything.

Olivia finally broke the silence. "Well, it's nice seeing you again. We are meeting my father down the road a little ways so we better get going."

"Okay. It was nice seeing you." Chris said.

Olivia hadn't been that uncomfortable in a long time. "That was so awkward." She said.

"Well at least I'm better looking." Avery said.

Olivia cracked up laughing. She loved his sense of humor. "Well, I'm glad that you see the silver lining in everything." She said as they walked hand in hand on down the road.

They watched the parade and when it was all over, they met up with David to discuss the annual Thanksgiving Day feast that he sponsored for the homeless.

"Avery." David said. "This will be your first year to do this. Every year we do a huge Thanksgiving Dinner for the homeless. This is something that Olivia's mom started years ago. We cook up turkeys, potatoes, macaroni and cheese. You name it we cook it. The town people get together and drop off desserts and dishes and it's a huge success. You will enjoy it."

"I can't wait." Avery said.

Olivia said. "I'll make a list and go to the stores and see who wants to donate things and then I'll buy what we can't get donated. I'll get with Mrs. Peterson too. She helps every year."

"Sounds good." David said.

When they were all done with the planning Olivia gave her dad a kiss on the cheek and her and Avery left.

When they got in the car Avery turned to Olivia. "It was an interesting day. Are you okay?"

Olivia knew he was talking about Chris. "It was awkward seeing Chris but we have all moved on. That seems like a lifetime ago."

Avery took her hand in his. "I love you."

When they got home, they walked in and took their coats off. Olivia thought Avery was being kind of quiet. "Is everything okay. You seem quiet. Is it seeing Chris today?"

Avery looked up. He hadn't noticed he had zoned out for a minute. "Oh no. That's no big deal but I do want to talk to you about something."
Olivia was a little bit worried. "Okay. Should I be worried."
Avery smiled. "Of course not. I just want to talk to you about something."
"Okay." Olivia said as she walked over to the couch to sit and brace herself for bad news."
Avery walked over and sat down beside her and took her hand in his. "Olivia. I love you. I love you more than anything in this world. We started out our relationship on this crazy whirl wind agenda. When I married you, I married you because I loved you, but it was all a show for the town. I want to ask you to renew our vows privately just you and me. We can go to Las

Vegas if you want. But a ceremony to say we love each other for no other reason than we love each other."

Olivia was speechless. She sat there with her mouth open but not being able to say anything. Tears trickled out of her eye. "Yes of course. Lets' go right now."

Avery laughed. He grabbed her and pulled her into him. He kissed her gently on the lips as he held her close.

They flew to Las Vegas the next day and did exactly that and then flew back before anyone knew they were gone. It wasn't about a public show. It was about them giving themselves their own start over.

The next few days Olivia walked around on cloud nine. She couldn't stop smiling. She also had a lot of stuff to get done for the Thanksgiving dinner. She ran to the store and picked up several ingredients to start getting some baking done.

Avery walked in from work to a kitchen full of flour containers, egg cartons, milk, and chocolate. The counter tops were overflowing. "Is there anything I can help you with?" He asked as he looked around the room.

Olivia was wearing a pink apron trimmed in white lace. "Sure. If you want to. I'm in the middle of working on desserts. I have several pies and cakes over there and a couple in the oven a couple more ready for the oven." She was rambling as she tended to do when she took on more than she could handle.

"Okay. Okay. It's no big deal. I helped my grandma in the kitchen lots of times. I'll get started wrapping all of the things you have done so they don't get hard. Then I'll move on to the next thing on the list."

Olivia couldn't help but love him. He was always there when she needed him the most. It took most of the night but they got all the baking done. When the last pie was wrapped and packed, she took her apron off and tossed it on the counter.

"I'm beat." She said. "Tomorrow is going to be a long day."

Avery took her hand softly in his. "Let's go on to bed. We'll get up early and get everything packed in the car and head over to the center to start setting up."

The next morning Olivia woke before Avery and she went to jump in the shower. She walked in the bathroom and stepped under the hot water. She leaned her head back and soaked it all in while lathering herself up. She really didn't want to get out but knew she had to. The civic center would be full of hungry people before noon. She had to get the food all set up. She got out, dried off and started dressing when she heard Avery stirring around in the other room.

He walked in rubbing his eyes and yawning. "How can you be up and all bright eyed and ready?"

Olivia laughed. "Trust me I'm not. I would love to be back in bed for a few more hours but we can't do that." She lightly kissed him. "Now move that cute butt of yours. We've got to go in less than thirty minutes."

Avery laughed as he jumped in the shower. He was in and out in less than five minutes. He just needed a quick wake up.

They packed the truck and drove over to the civic center. It was full of volunteers already. Olivia could tell it was going to be a good day. They got all the food set up and the doors opened right on time. The people filled the room, ate, and enjoyed the day. When it was all finished the cleaning crew began their work.

Chapter Eight

The holidays were fast approaching and Christmas was upon them. Olivia loved Christmas. It was her favorite holiday. She couldn't wait to decorate the house with colorful lights. She always went with the fake Christmas tree because she liked to put it up early and with a real tree she would have to wait. She went to the store and bought the biggest tree they had and filled the truck with enough decorations for ten houses but she knew she would find a place for each and every one of them. She had bought large toy soldiers to put on each side of the tree, a traditional nut cracker, and more lights than she would ever need including outside decorations as well.

Avery got home from work to a huge mess in the living room floor. "What is all this?"

"It's Christmas." Olivia said as she pretended to bat her eyes at him."

He couldn't help but laugh. "Oh, and you think the batting of a few eyelashes is going to get me to help you with all this mess."

"I was hoping yes."

Avery looked around the room at all the boxes she had out. "Where do you want me to start?" He asked. He never could tell her no.

Olivia jumped up and made her way around the mess to him. "I love you." She said. "First let's eat. I have dinner ready. I was just waiting on you to get home before I ate."

She walked into the kitchen and got out the roast she had been cooking all day. She put it on a white oval platter and surrounded it with potatoes and carrots. She sat it on the table and then went back for the garlic bread she made and then poured them both a glass of sweet tea.

"This looks great and smells delicious." Avery said as he sat down to eat.

"Thanks. It's a new recipe I'm trying out."

When they were all finished eating Olivia went back to her decorating. She wanted the house to be festive.

Olivia spent the next few days going from store-to-store shopping. She loved doing all the rituals even though buying her father a gift was probably the hardest thing in the world to do. She also needed to buy toys for the toy drive. She made sure each year that as many kids as she could would end up with presents that they wouldn't have had otherwise.

Olivia saw Andrea standing outside of one of the stores getting ready to get into a line to get a hotdog from the cart. "Hey Andrea."

Andrea glanced up and smiled. "Hey Olivia. What are you doing?"

"Getting some Christmas shopping done. Why don't you come to lunch with me instead of grabbing a hot dog."

Andrea walked over to her. "Sure. Sounds like fun. I've been so busy lately it will be nice to sit down and catch up."

"Great. Let's go to the Italian restaurant over there." They walked in and waited to be seated. When the hostess came over they followed her to their seat.

Olivia started looking at the menu. "I'm starving today. I ran out of the house without breakfast today."

"I haven't had anything today either." Andrea said. She picked up the napkin and rolled it around in her fingers.

Olivia looked over at her. "What's wrong? You seem upset?"

"Nothing I'm fine." Andrea said. As she looked around for the waiter.

"Andrea you are not fine. I've known you my entire life. I know when you are lying. So, spill it."

Before she could say anything, the waiter came to the table. "Are you ready to order?"

Olivia said. "Yes, we are. I would like the macaroni and cheese topped with grilled chicken, some breadsticks and a Caesar salad on the side."

The waiter wrote it all down and turned to Andrea.

"I'll have the same please."

Olivia knew there was something wrong. "Okay what is it?"

Andrea hesitated a bit. "Okay you know my dreams of wanting to open a coffee shop?"
"Yes. What about it?"
"Well I found the perfect location downtown. I went to the bank with my business plan and everything all lined out and they denied the loan. They said I don't have enough credit and I don't have a cosigner so they couldn't give me the money."

Olivia thought for a minute. "I see. I like your idea and I think you have a good business head on your shoulders. Have you thought about bringing on a partner?"

Andrea picked up a lemon and put it in her tea. She stirred it around with her spoon before picking it up to take a drink. "I don't know anyone that would be interested in partnering up on this. It's been my dream for years and I really think I could make a go of it but without the extra money I don't have enough saved."

The waiter came with their food and sat it down in front of them.

Olivia took a bite of her food and then looked at Andrea. "I might know somebody that would be interested and has the money to be a full partner."

Andrea almost dropped her fork. "What? Who?"

Olivia laughed. "Me. I would love to help you and I would love to be your partner."

Andrea didn't know what to say. "I can't believe this is happening. When I left the bank today, I had no idea where to go next. Then I run into you and my whole life changed in split second over mac and cheese."

Olivia couldn't help but laugh. "Remember when we were younger and every time, we had boy troubles my mom would make us mac and cheese." Olivia smiled as she thought back to her childhood.

Olivia paid the bill and left a tip and the two women walked out together. When they got outside Olivia turned to Andrea. "I have some more shopping to do. What about you? Do you want to go?"

Andrea said. "Yes, I need to walk off some of this food."

After a long day in town Olivia was ready to get home. She walked in and found Avery sitting on the couch watching tv.

He looked up as she walked in and saw all the bags in her hands. He jumped up and ran to help her. "Wow! Did you leave anything in the store?" He joked.

"Funny. I have some news to share with you. I ran into Andrea today."
"Oh yeah?"
"Yeah. This is going to be way out of left field here but I'm going into business with her."

"Yes, that is way out of left field. But that's what I love about you. What kind of business?"

Olivia told him all about their ideas and plans. She was actually getting excited about it the more she talked about it.

"It sounds like a great thing. I'm happy for you." He pulled her into him and kissed her gently on the forehead and then slowly moved to her lips.

It had been a long day and Olivia was ready for to call it a night.

As the days went by Olivia began to start feeling sick to her stomach. She wasn't sure exactly what was wrong but she knew for the past few days she hadn't felt very well so she decided to make a doctor's appointment.

Olivia sat in the examination room waiting for the doctor to come in. She had already done all of the tests with the nurse and was nervous about the results. She sat looking through old magazines not really reading the articles but needed something to focus her attention on.

The doctor knocked on the door before coming in. "Hello Olivia."

"Hello. Do you have results for me? Do you know why I've been feeling so sick lately? I'm sure it's nothing. I've been really busy lately starting a new business and the holidays. I'm sure I just over done it" She always rambled when she was nervous.

The doctor glanced at the chart and back to Olivia. She smiled. "Yes. Everything is fine. I have good news for you. You are pregnant."

Olivia looked up. "What? Really?"

"Yes. Your tests came back positive."

Olivia was speechless. She was having Avery's baby. She was over the moon with excitement.

After she left the doctor's office Olivia stopped off at the store to buy a card for Avery. She couldn't wait to give him his present. She drove home with a smile from ear to ear.

Avery walked in from work on Christmas Eve to her standing in front of him with a card. "What's this?" He asked.

"I can't wait. I want you to open my present to you now. I can't wait one more day."

Avery laughed and set his coat down. He opened the card and read "Merry Christmas Daddy." He looked up at Olivia confused.

She said. "I'm pregnant."
Avery lifted her up in his arms. "I love you."

Sometimes when you think you want something life finds a way of showing you what you need.

The End

9 798822 071705